SHOCK-HEADED PETER

in

LATIN - ENGLISH - GERMAN

in Latin by Peter Wiesmann
Petrus Hirsutus

in English: Anonymous Standard English Version
Shock-Headed Peter

from the original German by Heinrich Hoffmann
Der Struwwelpeter

Afterword by Walter Sauer

and a new English translation *Scruffypete* by Ann E. Wild

Bolchazy-Carducci Publishers, Inc.
Wauconda, Illinois USA (2002)

This publication was made possible by
PEGASUS LIMITED

Shock-Headed Peter in Latin — English — German
Petrus Hirsutus / Der Struwwelpeter

General Editor: Laurie Haight Keenan

Graphics: Philipp Sauer

BOLCHAZY-CARDUCCI PUBLISHERS, INC.
1000 Brown Street, Unit 101
Wauconda, Illinois 60084 U.S.A.
www.bolchazy.com

International Standard Book Number:
0-86516-548-3

Printed in the United States of America
2002
by Walsworth Publishing Co.

Latin Translation: Peter Wiesmann
Petrus Hirsutus: vel fabulae iocosae lepidis imagunculis
St. Gallen: Tschudy, 1954 with permission
English Translation: Anonymous Standard English Edition

German: Original German Version by Heinrich Hoffmann
Der Struwwelpeter: Lustige Geschichten und drollige Bilder
Frankfurt a. M.: Rütten & Loening (31st edition), 1861

Library of Congress Cataloging-in-Publication Data

Hoffmann, Heinrich, 1809-1894.
  [Struwwelpeter. English, German & Latin.]
  Petrus Hirsutus : vel fabulae iocosae lepidis imagunculis =
Shock-headed Peter / Heinrich Hoffmann ; Latin translation by Peter
Wiesmann ; afterword by Walter Sauer.
       p. cm.
Rhyming Latin translation, with original German text and popular English
translation on facing pages ; additional English translation by Ann E.
Wild precedes the afterword.
Summary: A collection of cautionary tales featuring the misadventures of
such characters as Shock-headed Peter, Cruel Frederick, Little Suck-a
Thumb, the Inky Boys, and Fidgety Philip.
  ISBN 0-86516-548-3
  [1. Behavior--Fiction. 2. Stories in rhyme. 3. Polyglot materials.] I.
Title: Shock-headed Peter. II. Wiesmann, Peter, 1904- III. Sauer,
Walter. IV. Title.

PZ10.5.H64 Pe 2002
[E]--dc21

                                                    2002009473

❧ Contents ❧

The English Struwwelpeter or Pretty Stories and Funny Pictures
Der Struwwelpeter oder lustige Geschichten und drollige Bilder
Petrus Hirsutus vel fabulae iocosae lepidis imagunculis

Foreword

When the children have been good,
That is, be it understood,
Good at meal-times, good at play,
Good all night and good all day –
They shall have the pretty things
Merry Christmas always brings.
Naughty, romping girls and boys
Tear their clothes and make a noise,
Spoil their pinafores and frocks,
And deserve no Christmas-box.
Such as these shall never look
At this pretty Picture-Book.

❧   ❧   ❧

Vorwort

Wenn die Kinder artig sind,
kommt zu ihnen das Christkind;
wenn sie ihre Suppe essen
und das Brot auch nicht vergessen,
wenn sie, ohne Lärm zu machen,
still sind bei den Siebensachen,
beim Spaziergehn auf den Gassen
von Mama sich führen lassen,
bringt es ihnen Gut's genug
und ein schönes Bilderbuch.

Praefatio

Favet liberis modestis
angelus diebus festis.
Iure si probi fruentur,
panem non obliviscentur,
si tranquilli residebunt,
cum deliciis manebunt,
matri manum offerent,
cum in viis ambulent,
librum afferct amatum
imagunculis ornatum.

Shock-Headed Peter

Just look at him! There he stands,
With his nasty hair and hands.
See! his nails are never cut;
They are grimed as black as soot;
And the sloven, I declare,
Never once has combed his hair;
Anything to me is sweeter
Than to see Shock-headed Peter.

৵ ৵ ৵

Der Struwwelpeter

Sieh einmal, hier steht er,
pfui! der Struwwelpeter!
An den Händen beiden
ließ er sich nicht schneiden
seine Nägel fast ein Jahr;
kämmen ließ er nicht sein Haar.
"Pfui!" ruft da ein jeder:
"Garstger Struwwelpeter!"

De Petro hirsuto

Hic est constitutus
Petrus, phui, hirsutus.
Semper erat idem:
Ne quotannis quidem
ungues recidebat
crines nec pectebat.
"Phui," vocamus, "tetrum
hunc hirsutum Petrum!"

The Story of Cruel Frederick

Here is cruel Frederick, see!
A horrid wicked boy was he;
He caught the flies, poor little things,
And then tore off their tiny wings,
He killed the birds, and broke the chairs,
And threw the kitten down the stairs;
And oh! far worse than all beside,
He whipped his Mary, till she cried.

Die Geschichte vom bösen Friederich

Der Friederich, der Friederich,
das war ein arger Wüterich!
Er fing die Fliegen in dem Haus
und riß ihnen die Flügel aus.
Er schlug die Stühl und Vögel tot,
die Katzen litten große Not.
Und höre nur, wie bös er war:
Er peitschte seine Gretchen gar!

De Frederico maligno fabula

Eheu, nefarius ac scelestus
fuit Fredericus et funestus.
In muris muscas capiebat
eisque alas eripiebat.
Necabat sellas atque aves
et magna felium erat clades.
Quin Margaretam oppugnabat
nec non sororem flagellabat.

The trough was full, and faithful Tray
Came out to drink one sultry day;
He wagged his tail, and wet his lip,
When cruel Fred snatched up a whip,
And whipped poor Tray till he was sore,
And kicked and whipped him more and more:
At this, good Tray grew very red,
And growled, and bit him till he bled;
Then you should only have been by,
To see how Fred did scream and cry!

ॐ ॐ ॐ

Am Brunnen stand ein großer Hund,
trank Wasser dort mit seinem Mund.
Da mit der Peitsch herzu sich schlich
der bitterböse Friederich;
und schlug den Hund, der heulte sehr,
und trat und schlug ihn immer mehr.
Da biß der Hund ihn in das Bein,
recht tief bis in das Blut hinein.
Der bitterböse Friederich,
der schrie und weinte bitterlich. –
Jedoch nach Hause lief der Hund
und trug die Peitsche in dem Mund.

Ad fontem quondam stat immanis
hauritque aquam lingua canis.
Tum Fredericus clam accessit,
in manibus flagellum gessit.

Canem ferit, etsi latrabat,
et magis iterum calcabat.
At canis crus corripuit
et cruor alte micuit
et Frederici pessimi
clamores sunt clarissimi.
Canis domum revertebatur,
in ore flagrum ferebatur.

So Frederick had to go to bed;
His leg was very sore and red!
The Doctor came and shook his head,
And made a very great to-do,
And gave him nasty physic too.

But good dog Tray is happy now;
He has no time to say "Bow-wow!"
He seats himself in Frederick's chair
And laughs to see the nice things there:
The soup he swallows, sup by sup –
And eats the pies and puddings up.

 ❧   ❧   ❧

Ins Bett muß Friedrich nun hinein,
litt vielen Schmerz an seinem Bein;
und der Herr Doktor sitzt dabei
und gibt ihm bittre Arzenei.

Der Hund an Friedrichs Tischchen saß,
wo er den großen Kuchen aß;
aß auch die gute Leberwurst
und trank den Wein für seinen Durst.
Die Peitsche hat er mitgebracht
und nimmt sie sorglich sehr in acht.

Recondunt puerum in lectum
magnis doloribus affectum.
Cubili medicus adstabat,
amarum medicamen dabat.

In sella canis residebat
et libum eius comedebat
hepaticumque botulum,
bibebat vini poculum.
Flagellum secum afferebat
et diligenter custodiebat.

The Dreadful Story about Harriet and the Matches

It almost makes me cry to tell
What foolish Harriet befell.
Mamma and Nurse went out one day
And left her all alone at play;
Now, on the table close at hand,
A box of matches chanced to stand;
And kind Mamma and Nurse had told her,
That, if she touched them, they would scold her.
But Harriet said "O, what a pity!
For, when they burn, it is so pretty;
They crackle so, and spit, and flame;
Mamma, too, often does the same."

The pussy-cats heard this,
And they began to hiss,
And stretch their claws,
And raise their paws;
"Me-ow" they said, "me-ow, me-o,
You'll burn to death, if you do so."

ᏊᏊ ᏊᏊ ᏊᏊ

Die gar traurige Geschichte mit dem Feuerzeug

Paulinchen war allein zu Haus,
die Eltern waren beide aus.
Als sie nun durch das Zimmer sprang
mit leichtem Mut und Sing und Sang,
da sah sie plötzlich vor sich stehn
ein Feuerzeug, nett anzusehn.
"Ei", sprach sie, "ei, wie schön und fein!
Das muß ein trefflich Spielzeug sein.
Ich zünde mir ein Hölzchen an,
wie's oft die Mutter hat getan."

Und Minz und Maunz, die Katzen,
erheben ihre Tatzen.
Sie drohen mit den Pfoten:
"Der Vater hat's verboten!
Miau! Mio! Miau! Mio!
Laß stehn! Sonst brennst du lichterloh!"

De flammiferis
fabula tristissima

Paulina domi parentibus
relicta est absentibus.
Cum per conclave autem iret
et cantu hilari saliret,
conspexit illa misera
in mensula flammifera.
"Pol," inquit, "istae virgulae
mihi erunt deliciae!
Unam incendere conabor
et matrem meam imitabor."

Affectae autem magna cura
tollebant feles sua crura,
sublatis pedibus monebant:
"Vetabat pater," vagiebant,
"interitum tibi parabis!
Ne moveas! Nam deflagrabis!"

But Harriet would not take advice:
She lit a match, it was so nice!
It crackled so, it burned so clear –
Exactly like the picture here.
She jumped for joy and ran about
And was too pleased to put it out.

The pussy-cats saw this
And said "Oh, naughty, naughty Miss!"
And stretched their claws,
And raised their paws:
"'Tis very, very wrong, you know,
Me-ow, me-o, me-ow, me-o,
You will be burnt, if you do so."

Paulinchen hört die Katzen nicht!
Das Hölzchen brennt gar hell und licht,
das flackert lustig, knistert laut,
grad wie ihr's auf dem Bilde schaut.
Paulinchen aber freut sich sehr
und sprang im Zimmer hin und her.

Doch Minz und Maunz, die Katzen,
erheben ihre Tatzen.
Sie drohen mit den Pfoten:
"Die Mutter hat's verboten!
Miau! Mio! Miau! Mio!
Wirf's weg! Sonst brennst du lichterloh!"

Paulina aures non praebebat.
Lignum clarissime fulgebat.
Nam crepat flamma tremula:
Vides in imaguncula.
Saltabat cum laetitia
illuc et huc per atria.

Affectae autem magna cura
tollebant feles sua crura,
sublatis pedibus monebant:
"Vetabat mater," vagiebant,
"interitum tibi parabis!
Abicias! Nam deflagrabis!"

And see! Oh, what a dreadful thing!
The fire has caught her apron-string;
Her apron burns, her arms, her hair;
She burns all over everywhere.

Then how the pussy-cats did mew,
What else, poor pussies, could they do?
They screamed for help, 'twas all in vain!
So then, they said, "We'll scream again;
Make haste, make haste, me-ow, me-o,
She'll burn to death, we told her so."

∾   ∾   ∾

Doch, weh! die Flamme faßt das Kleid,
die Schürze brennt; es leuchtet weit.
Es brennt die Hand, es brennt das Haar,
es brennt das ganze Kind sogar.

Und Minz und Maunz, die schreien
gar jämmerlich zu zweien:
"Herbei! Herbei! Wer hilft geschwind?
In Feuer steht das ganze Kind!
Miau! Mio! Miau! Mio!
Zu Hilf! Das Kind brennt lichterloh!"

Vae! Flamma tunicam capessit
et praecinctorium ardescit,
manus, crinis exuritur,
puella quin corripitur!

Amborum felium vagitus
est miserabilis auditus:
"Quis opem fert celeriter?
Deflagrat nunc crudeliter!
Venite huic auxilio,
nam deflagrat incendio!"

So she was burnt, with all her clothes,
And arms, and hands, and eyes, and nose;
Till she had nothing more to lose
Except her little scarlet shoes;
And nothing else but these was found
Among her ashes on the ground.

And when the good cats sat beside
The smoking ashes, how they cried!
"Me-ow, me-oo, me-ow, me-oo,
What will Mamma and Nursy do?"
Their tears ran down their cheeks so fast,
They made a little pond at last.

Verbrannt ist alles ganz und gar,
das arme Kind mit Haut und Haar;
ein Häuflein Asche blieb allein,
und beide Schuh, so hübsch und fein.

Und Minz und Maunz, die kleinen,
die sitzen da und weinen:
"Miau! Mio! Miau! Mio!
Wo sind die armen Eltern? Wo?"
Und ihre Tränen fließen
wie's Bächlein auf den Wiesen.

Paulinam flamma usserat,
puellae nil supererat
acervus nisi cineris
cum rubris soleis pauperis.

Sed parvae feles adsidebant
ac eiulantes ambo flebant:
"Ubi terrarum" vagientes,
"estis miserrimi parentes?"
Earum lacrimae fluunt,
ut rivuli in pratis sunt.

The Story of the Inky Boys

As he had often done before,
The woolly-headed black-a-moor
One nice fine summer's day went out
To see the shops and walk about;
And as he found it hot, poor fellow,
He took with him his green umbrella.
Then Edward, little noisy wag,
Ran out and laughed, and waved his flag;
And William came in jacket trim
And brought his wooden hoop with him;
And Arthur, too, snatched up his toys
And joined the other naughty boys.
So, one and all set up a roar,
And laughed and hooted more and more,
And kept on singing, – only think! –
"Oh! Blacky, you're as black as ink."

ᔆ   ᔆ   ᔆ

Die Geschichte von den schwarzen Buben

Es ging spazieren vor dem Tor
ein kohlpechrabenschwarzer Mohr.
Die Sonne schien ihm auf's Gehirn,
da nahm er seinen Sonnenschirm.
Da kam der Ludwig hergerannt
und trug sein Fähnchen in der Hand.
Der Kaspar kam mit schnellem Schritt
und brachte seine Brezel mit;
und auch der Wilhelm war nicht steif
und brachte seinen runden Reif.
Die schrien und lachten alle drei,
als dort das Mohrchen ging vorbei,
weil es so schwarz wie Tinte sei!

De pueris denigratis fabula

It ante portam ambulatum
nigerrimus caput atratum.
Quod sole eius frons torretur,
umbella calor amovetur.
Heus, Ludovicum, ecce illum!
in manu tenet is vexillum.
Casparus accurrit cum spira
et is celeritate mira.
Delectat trochus nobilem
Gulielmum haud immobilem.
Hi omnes tres rident clamantes
praetereuntem adspectantes,
os illudebant illius,
quod atramento nigrius.

Now tall Agrippa lived close by –
So tall, he almost touched the sky;
He had a mighty inkstand too,
In which a great goose-feather grew;
He called out in an angry tone
"Boys, leave the black-a-moor alone!
For if he tries with all his might,
He cannot change from black to white."
But ah! they did not mind a bit
What great Agrippa said of it;
But went on laughing, as before,
And hooting at the black-a-moor.

૭ૂ ૭ૂ ૭ૂ

Da kam der große Nikolas
mit seinem großen Tintenfaß.
Der sprach: "Ihr Kinder, hört mir zu,
und laßt den Mohren hübsch in Ruh!
Was kann denn dieser Mohr dafür,
daß er so weiß nicht ist wie ihr?"
Die Buben aber folgten nicht
und lachten ihm ins Angesicht
und lachten ärger als zuvor
über den armen schwarzen Mohr.

Advenit nunc in hoc momento
Nicolaus cum atramento.
"O pueri," dixit, "pareatis,
hunc Maurum ne irrideatis!
Ne afficiatis hunc dolore,
quod non eodem est colore!"
At pueri non oboedientes
pudorem nullum sentientes
maiore gaudio ridebant,
quod nigrum parvulum videbant.

Then great Agrippa foams with rage –
Look at him on this very page!
He seizes Arthur, seizes Ned,
Takes William by his little head;
And they may scream and kick and call,
Into the ink he dips them all;
Into the inkstand, one, two, three,
Till they are black, as black can be:
Turn over now, and you shall see.

Der Niklas wurde bös und wild, –
du siehst es hier auf diesem Bild!
Er packte gleich die Buben fest,
beim Arm, beim Kopf, bei Rock und West',
den Wilhelm und den Ludewig,
den Kaspar auch, der wehrte sich.
Er tunkt sie in die Tinte tief,
wie auch der Kaspar: "Feuer!" rief.
Bis übern Kopf ins Tintenfaß
tunkt sie der große Nikolas.

Nicolaus furore victus
in hac imagine est pictus:
Corripiebat tunc malignos
gravissimaque poena dignos
et Ludovicum et Casparum,
Gulielmum quoque haud ignarum.
Quin etiam mergit delinquentes
in cupam valde resistentes.
In atramento universi
sunt mali pueri submersi.

See, there they are, and there they run!
The black-a-moor enjoys the fun.
They have been made as black as crows,
Quite black all over, eyes and nose,
And legs, and arms, and heads, and toes,
And trousers, pinafores, and toys –
The silly little inky boys!
Because they set up such a roar,
And teased the harmless black-a-moor.

❦   ❦   ❦

Du siehst sie hier, wie schwarz sie sind,
viel schwärzer als das Mohrenkind!
der Mohr voraus im Sonnenschein,
die Tintenbuben hintendrein;
und hätten sie nicht so gelacht,
hätt' Niklas sie nicht schwarz gemacht.

Videre licet irrisores
hic aliquanto nigriores.
Sol fulget capiti atrati,
eum sequuntur denigrati;
et nisi Maurum irrisissent,
hanc poenam gravem vitavissent.

The Story of the Man that Went out Shooting

This is the man that shoots the hares;
This is the coat he always wears:
With game-bag, powder-horn and gun
He's going out to have some fun.

He finds it hard, without a pair
Of spectacles, to shoot the hare.
The hare sits snug in leaves and grass,
And laughs to see the green man pass.

           ❦   ❦   ❦

Die Geschichte vom wilden Jäger

Es zog der wilde Jägersmann
sein grasgrün neues Röcklein an;
nahm Ranzen, Pulverhorn und Flint'
und lief hinaus ins Feld geschwind.

Er trug die Brille auf der Nas'
und wollte schießen tot den Has.
Das Häschen sitzt im Blätterhaus
und lacht den blinden Jäger aus.

De saevo venatore fabula

Venator saevus et astutus
et vestem viridem indutus
peram et arma tum captavit
et perspicillum applicavit
ad nasum, campum invasurus
necem lepusculo laturus.

Lepus in foliis sedebat,
inopinantem irridebat.

Now, as the sun grew very hot,
And he a heavy gun had got,
He lay down underneath a tree
And went to sleep, as you may see.
And, while he slept like any top,
The little hare came, hop, hop, hop,
Took gun and spectacles, and then
On her hind legs went off again.

୨୦   ୨୦   ୨୦

Jetzt schien die Sonne gar zu sehr,
da ward ihm sein Gewehr zu schwer.
Er legte sich ins grüne Gras;
das alles sah der kleine Has.
Und als der Jäger schnarcht' und schlief,
der Has ganz heimlich zu ihm lief
und nahm die Flint' und auch die Brill',
und schlich davon ganz leis und still.

Quod sol fervebat ista hora,
fiebant arma graviora.
In herbis ergo recumbebat,
id quod lepusculus videbat.
Venator stertit dormiens,
cum lepus clam progrediens
et arma haec cum perspicillo
corripit et fugit tranquillo.

The green man wakes and sees her place
The spectacles upon her face;
And now she's trying all she can,
To shoot the sleepy, green-coat man.
He cries and screams and runs away;
The hare runs after him all day
And hears him call out everywhere:
"Help! Fire! Help! The Hare! The Hare!"

      ॐ   ॐ   ॐ

Die Brille hat das Häschen jetzt
sich selber auf die Nas' gesetzt,
und schießen will's aus dem Gewehr.
Der Jäger aber fürcht' sich sehr.
Er läuft davon und springt und schreit:
"Zu Hilf, ihr Leut! Zu Hilf, ihr Leut!"

Quo perspicillo oculi
muniti sunt lepusculi.
Tum armis eum appetebat,
venator autem timescebat,
effugit clamans: "Obsecro!
Succurrite mi misero!"

At last he stumbled at the well,
Head over ears, and in he fell.
The hare stopped short, took aim, and hark!
Bang went the gun – she missed her mark!

The poor man's wife was drinking up
Her coffee in her coffee-cup;
The gun shot cup and saucer through;
"O dear!" cried she, "what shall I do?"
There lived close by the cottage there
The hare's own child, the little hare;
And while she stood upon her toes,
The coffee fell and burned her nose.
"O dear!" she cried, with spoon in hand,
"Such fun I do not understand."

❧   ❧   ❧

Da kommt der wilde Jägersmann
zuletzt beim tiefen Brünnchen an.
Er springt hinein. Die Not war groß;
es schießt der Has die Flinte los.

Des Jägers Frau am Fenster saß
und trank aus ihrer Kaffeetass'.
Die schoß das Häschen ganz entzwei;
da rief die Frau: "O wei! O wei!"
Doch bei dem Brünnchen heimlich saß
des Häschens Kind, der kleine Has.
Der hockte da im grünen Gras;
dem floß der Kaffee auf die Nas'.
Er schrie: "Wer hat mich da verbrannt?"
und hielt den Löffel in der Hand.

Venator summa vi currebat,
in puteum se proiciebat.
Nam summum fuit periculum:
Lepus emisit iaculum.

Sed post fenestram, en eam!
Est coniux sorbens coffeam.
Quo ictu autem testa fracta
"Vae" clamat uxor timefacta.
Ad fontem sedit illius
lepusculi clam filius.
Erat in foliis submersus
ac nasus coffea adspersus.
"Quis est," exclamat, "qui me urit?"
Et cochleari valde furit.

The Story of Little Suck-a-Thumb

One day, Mamma said, "Conrad dear,
I must go out and leave you here.
But mind now, Conrad, what I say,
Don't suck your thumb while I'm away.
The great tall tailor always comes
To little boys who suck their thumbs;
And ere they dream what he's about,
He take his great sharp scissors out
And cuts their thumbs clean off – and then,
You know, they never grow again."

Mamma had scarcely turned her back,
The thumb was in, Alack! Alack!

☙   ☙   ☙

Die Geschichte vom Daumenlutscher

"Konrad!" sprach die Frau Mama,
"ich geh aus und du bleibst da.
Sei hübsch ordentlich und fromm,
bis nach Haus ich wieder komm.
Und vor allem, Konrad, hör!
lutsche nicht am Daumen mehr;
denn der Schneider mit der Scher'
kommt sonst ganz geschwind daher,
und die Daumen schneidet er
ab, als ob Papier es wär."

Fort geht nun die Mutter, und
wupp! den Daumen in den Mund.

De puero, qui pollices sugebat, fabula

"Tu, Conrade, mi parebis,
me absente remanebis!"
dixit mater, "dum sum foris,
opto, sis modesti moris.
Audi tu, Conrade, imprimis:
pollices ne sugas nimis!
Nam cum forfice venturum
pollicesque resecturum
vestificum, ut papyrum,
tibi dico, – non est mirum!"

Mater clausit ianuam,
denuo puer sugit iam!

The door flew open, in he ran,
The great, long, red-legged scissor-man.
Oh! children, see! the tailor's come
And caught out little Suck-a-Thumb.
Snip! Snap! Snip! the scissors go;
And Conrad cries out, "Oh! Oh! Oh!"
Snip! Snap! Snip! They go so fast,
That both his thumbs are off at last.

Mamma comes home: there Conrad stands,
And looks quite sad, and shows his hands;
"Ah!" said Mamma "I knew he'd come
To naughty little Suck-a-Thumb."

🙦   🙦   🙦

Bautz! da geht die Türe auf,
und herein in schnellem Lauf
springt der Schneider in die Stub'
zu dem Daumen-Lutscher-Bub.
Weh! Jetzt geht es klipp und klapp
mit der Scher' die Daumen ab,
mit der großen scharfen Scher'!
Hei! Da schreit der Konrad sehr.

Als die Mutter kommt nach Haus,
sieht der Konrad traurig aus.
Ohne Daumen steht er dort,
die sind alle beide fort.

Subito recluditur
porta et conspicitur
vestificus intraturus
pupulumque aggressurus.
Resecabat forfice
digitos horrifice
pueri, qui trepidabat
misereque eiulabat.

Vidit mater, cum redit,
interim quid gestum sit.
Heu, Conradus mutilatus
stat pollicibus privatus.

The Story of Augustus, Who Would not Have Any Soup

Augustus was a chubby lad;
Fat ruddy cheeks Augustus had;
And everybody saw with joy
The plump and hearty, healthy boy.
He ate and drank as he was told,
And never let his soup get cold.
But one day, one cold winter's day,
He screamed out, "Take the soup away!
O take the nasty soup away!
I won't have any soup to-day."

৯৯   ৯৯   ৯৯

Die Geschichte vom Suppen-Kaspar

Der Kaspar, der war kerngesund,
ein dicker Bub und kugelrund,
er hatte Backen rot und frisch;
die Suppe aß er hübsch bei Tisch.
Doch einmal fing er an zu schrein:
"Ich esse keine Suppe! Nein!
Ich esse meine Suppe nicht!
Nein, meine Suppe eß ich nicht!"

De Casparo, qui iusculum edere nolebat, fabula

Casparus puer validus
fuit crassus neque pallidus,
rudebant valde eius genae,
intererat modeste cenae.
Sed quondam exclamat: "Non cedo!
Hoc malum iusculum non edo!
Non edo meum iusculum!
Non edo ullum frustulum!"

Next day, now look, the picture shows
How lank and lean Augustus grows!
Yet, though he feels so weak and ill,
The naughty fellow cries out still,
"Not any soup for me, I say:
O take the nasty soup away!
I won't have any soup to-day."

The third day comes: Oh what a sin!
To make himself so pale and thin.
Yet, when the soup is put on table,
He screams, as loud as he is able,
"Not any soup for me, I say:
O take the nasty soup away!
I won't have any soup to-day."

Look at him, now the fourth day's come!
He scarcely weighs a sugar-plum;
He's like a little bit of thread,
And on the fifth day, he was – dead!

Am nächsten Tag, – ja sieh nur her!
da war er schon viel magerer.
Da fing er wieder an zu schrein:
"Ich esse keine Suppe! Nein!
Ich esse meine Suppe nicht!
Nein, meine Suppe eß ich nicht!"

Am dritten Tag, o weh und ach!
wie ist der Kaspar dünn und schwach!
Doch als die Suppe kam herein,
gleich fing er wieder an zu schrein:
"Ich esse keine Suppe! Nein!
Ich esse meine Suppe nicht!
Nein, meine Suppe eß ich nicht!"

Am vierten Tage endlich gar
der Kaspar wie ein Fädchen war.
Er wog vielleicht ein halbes Lot, –
und war am fünften Tage tot.

Postridie eius diei
adspectus macrior est ei.
Tum clamat iterum: "Non cedo!
Hoc malum iusculum non edo!
Non edo meum iusculum!
Non edo ullum frustulum!"

Sed tertio die corpus eius
debilius fit atque peius.
At ubi cibi apponuntur,
clamores eius audiuntur,
quos tollit denuo: "Non cedo!
Hoc malum iusculum non edo!
Non edo meum iusculum!
Non edo ullum frustulum!"

Et quarto die fuit nilum
Casparus autem nisi filum.
Semuncialis tunc fuit
et quinto mortem obiit.

The Story of Fidgety Philip

"Let me see if Philip can
Be a little gentleman;
Let me see, if he is able
To sit still for once at table":
Thus Papa bade Phil behave;
And Mamma looked very grave.
But fidgety Phil,
He won't sit still;
He wriggles,
And giggles,
And then, I declare,
Swings backwards and forwards
And tilts up his chair,
Just like any rocking horse –
"Philip! I am getting cross!"

ഐ   ഐ   ഐ

Die Geschichte vom Zappel-Philipp

"Ob der Philipp heute still
wohl bei Tische sitzen will?"
Also sprach in ernstem Ton
der Papa zu seinem Sohn,
und die Mutter blickte stumm
auf dem ganzen Tisch herum.
Doch der Philipp hörte nicht,
was zu ihm der Vater spricht.
      Er gaukelt
      und schaukelt,
      er trappelt
      und zappelt
auf dem Stuhle hin und her.
"Philipp, das mißfällt mir sehr!"

De Philippo oscillante fabula

"Nonne placidus sedebit
hodie filius, ut decebit?"
Sic Philippo ait in cena
pater voce haud serena.
Mater vultum non deflexit,
muta mensam circumspexit.
Puer autem neglegebat
verba, quae parens dicebat.
Crura movet trepidans,
sedet in sella oscillans
huc, illuc. "Videlicet!
Mi Philippe, displicet!"

See the naughty, restless child
Growing still more rude and wild,
Till his chair falls over quite.
Philip screams with all his might,
Catches at the cloth, but then
That makes matters worse again.
Down upon the ground they fall,
Glasses, plates, knives, forks, and all.
How Mamma did fret and frown,
When she saw them tumbling down!
And Papa made such a face!
Philip is in sad disgrace.

ℂ ℂ ℂ

Seht, ihr lieben Kinder, seht,
wie's dem Philipp weiter geht!
Oben steht es auf dem Bild.
Seht! Er schaukelt gar zu wild,
bis der Stuhl nach hinten fällt;
da ist nichts mehr, was ihn hält;
nach dem Tischtuch greift er, schreit.
Doch was hilft's? Zu gleicher Zeit
fallen Teller, Flasch' und Brot,
Vater ist in großer Not,
und die Mutter blicket stumm
auf dem ganzen Tisch herum.

Adspiciatis immodestum,
quidnam postea sit gestum.
Est depictus: Insolenter
oscillat, quam vehementer!
Sic, ut sella delabatur.
Non est, quo retineatur.
Arripit mantelium.
Nusquam est auxilium.
Cadunt panis et catilla,
pater frustra tenet illa.
Mater vultum non deflexit,
muta mensam circumspexit.

Whe hilip, where is he?
Fairl red up you see!
Clot all are lying on him;
He julled down all upon him.
Wh errible to-do!
Dis glasses, snapt in two!
He knife, and there a fork!
Ph this is cruel work.
Ta all so bare, and ah!
Pr Papa, and poor Mamma
L quite cross, and wonder how
Ty shall have their dinner now.

Nun ist Philipp ganz versteckt,
und der Tisch ist abgedeckt.
was der Vater essen wollt',
unten auf der Erde rollt;
Suppe, Brot und alle Bissen,
alles ist herabgerissen;
Suppenschüssel ist entzwei,
und die Eltern stehn dabei.
Beide sind gar zornig sehr,
haben nichts zu essen mehr.

Mensa tum detegitur,
filius obruitur.
Cibus, quem parens edebat,
humi autem decidebat,
frusta, vinum, panis, ius
evertuntur funditus.
Humi patina est fracta,
cena subito peracta.
Parentesque stant irati,
cibis enim sunt privati.

The Story of Johnny Head-In-Air

As he trudged along to school,
It was always Johnny's rule
To be looking at the sky
And the clouds that floated by;
But what just before him lay,
In his way,
Johnny never thought about;
So that every one cried out,
"Look at little Johnny there,
Little Johnny Head-In-Air!"

Running just in Johnny's way
Came a little dog one day;
Johnny's eyes were still astray
Up on high,
In the sky;
And he never heard them cry,
"Johnny, mind, the dog is nigh!"
Bump!
Dump!
Down they fell, with such a thump,
Dog and Johnny in a lump!

Die Geschichte vom Hans Guck-in-die-Luft

Wenn der Hans zur Schule ging,
stets sein Blick am Himmel hing.
Nach den Dächern, Wolken, Schwalben
schaut er aufwärts, allenthalben:
vor die eignen Füße dicht,
ja, da sah der Bursche nicht,
also daß ein jeder ruft:
"Seht den Hans Guck-in-die-Luft!"

Kam ein Hund dahergerannt;
Hänslein blickte unverwandt
in die Luft.
Niemand ruft:
"Hans! gib acht, der Hund ist nah!"
Was geschah?
Pauz! Perdauz! – da liegen zwei!
Hund und Hänschen nebenbei.

De Iohanne, qui in aerem spectabat, fabula

Iohannes, cum in ludum ibat,
attentus esse tum nequibat
ad nubes mentem dirigens,
hirundines conspiciens
Quod pedibus eius subiacebat,
id puerum autem fugiebat,
ut luderent inopinantem
Iohannem aerem adspectantem.

Cum quondam oculos tollebat,
repente canis accurrebat.
Non erat quisquam, qui moneret,
prudenter canem ut caveret.
Fiebat, ut congrederentur,
canis puerque laberentur.

Once, with head as high as ever,
Johnny walked beside the river.
Johnny watched the swallows trying
Which was cleverest at flying.
Oh! what fun!
Johnny watched the bright round sun
Going in and coming out;
This was all he thought about.
So he strode on, only think!
To the river's very brink,
Where the bank was high and steep,
And the water very deep;
And the fishes, in a row,
Stared to see him coming so.

One step more! Oh! sad to tell!
Headlong in poor Johnny fell.
And the fishes, in dismay,
Wagged their tails and swam away.

Einst ging er an Ufers Rand
mit der Mappe in der Hand.
Nach dem blauen Himmel hoch
sah er, wo die Schwalbe flog,
also daß er kerzengrad
immer mehr zum Flusse trat.
Und die Fischlein in der Reih
sind erstaunt sehr, alle drei.

Noch ein Schritt! und plumps! der Hans
stürzt hinab kopfüber ganz! –
Die drei Fischlein sehr erschreckt
haben sich sogleich versteckt.

Ibat secundum ripulam,
in manu tenet capsulam.
Dum sursum tollit oculos
hirundinum in circulos,
medium in fluvii gurgitem
tulit pedem praecipitem.
Ac ordinatim pisces tres
admirabantur istas res.

Heus! Unum gradum addidit,
in fluvium cum incidit.
Sed pisces tres perterriti
in imum sunt reconditi.

There lay Johnny on his face,
With his nice red writing-case;
But, as they were passing by,
Two strong men had heard him cry;
And, with sticks, these two strong men
Hooked poor Johnny out again.

Oh! you should have seen him shiver
When they pulled him from the river.
He was in a sorry plight!
Dripping wet, and such a fright!
Wet all over, everywhere,
Clothes, and arms, and face, and hair:
Johnny never will forget
What it is to be so wet.

And the fishes, one, two, three,
Are come back again, you see;
Up they came the moment after,
To enjoy the fun and laughter.
Each popped out his little head,
And, to tease poor Johnny, said
"Silly little Johnny, look,
You have lost your writing-book!"

Doch zum Glück da kommen zwei
Männer aus der Näh herbei,
und die haben ihn mit Stangen
aus dem Wasser aufgefangen.

Seht! Nun steht er triefend naß!
Ei! das ist ein schlechter Spaß!
Wasser läuft dem armen Wicht
aus den Haaren ins Gesicht,
aus den Kleidern, von den Armen;
und es friert ihn zum Erbarmen.

Doch die Fischlein alle drei
schwimmen hurtig gleich herbei;
Strecken 's Köpflein aus der Flut,
lachen, daß man's hören tut,
lachen fort noch lange Zeit;
und die Mappe schwimmt schon weit.

Quod duo viri advenerunt,
qui casu procul haud fuerunt.
Iohannes contis erat captus,
in terram iterum retractus.

En! Madefactum videatis!
Mehercle, risum teneatis!
Demanat aqua crinibus
in faciem, ex vestibus,
de bracchiis. Puer friget,
illius omnes miseret.

Sed pisces tres communiter
adnatant nunc celeriter,
ex aquis caput porrigebant
magnaque voce irridebant.
Rident diutissime vi tota
capsa longissime remota.

The Story of Flying Robert

When the rain comes tumbling down
In the country or the town,
All good little girls and boys
Stay at home and mind their toys.
Robert thought "No, when it pours,
It is better out of doors."
Rain it did, and in a minute
Bob was in it.
Here you see him, silly fellow,
Underneath his red umbrella.

What a wind! Oh! how it whistles.
Through the trees and flowers and thistles!
It has caught his red umbrella:
Now look at him, silly fellow –
Up he flies
To the skies.
No one heard his screams and cries;
Through the clouds the rude wind bore him,
And his hat flew on before him.

Soon they got to such a height,
They were nearly out of sight!
And the hat went up so high,
That it nearly touched the sky.
No one ever yet could tell
Where they stopped, or where they fell:
Only this one thing is plain,
Bob was never seen again!

Die Geschichte vom fliegenden Robert

Wenn der Regen niederbraust,
wenn der Sturm das Feld durchsaust,
bleiben Mädchen oder Buben
hübsch daheim in ihren Stuben. –
Robert aber dachte: "Nein!
Das muß draußen herrlich sein!" –
Und im Felde patschet er
mit dem Regenschirm umher.

Hui, wie pfeift der Sturm und keucht,
daß der Baum sich niederbeugt!
Seht! den Schirm erfaßt der Wind,
und der Robert fliegt geschwind
durch die Luft so hoch, so weit;
Niemand hört ihn, wenn er schreit.
An die Wolken stößt er schon,
und der Hut fliegt auch davon.

Schirm und Robert fliegen dort
durch die Wolken immer fort.
Und der Hut fliegt weit voran,
stößt zuletzt am Himmel an.
Wo der Wind sie hingetragen,
ja! das weiß kein Mensch zu sagen.

De Roberto, qui per aerem volabat, fabula

Dum pluit cum strepitu,
ager sonat fremitu,
domi manent pueri
cum puellis integri.
Quod Roberto displicebat,
domum suam relinquebat
atque per diluvia
it cum parapluvia.

Stridet saeviens tempestas,
flectit arbores funestas.
Vide parapluviam:
Ventus tollit etiam,
en Robertum avolantem!
Nemo audit inclamantem.
Nubes ille attingebat
causiamque amittebat.

Tum per nubes vehitur,
puerum praegreditur
capitisque tegimentum.
Ille tangit firmamentum.
Quo hos ventus tulerit,
nullus homo dixerit!

Scruffypete

Translated by Ann Elizabeth Wild

Prologue

When the children are quite good
comes Saint Nicholas in his hood.
If they eat their soup all up,
eat their bread and drain their cup,
if they play without a noise
on the carpet with their toys,
and when walking in the street
keep quite close to Mummy's feet,
then he brings them goodies fine
and this storybook of mine.

≈   ≈   ≈   ≈   ≈   ≈   ≈   ≈   ≈

Scruffypete

He's steady on his feet,
the famous Scruffypete,
and from his hands he trails
ten lengthy fingernails.
To cutting he says, "No!"
To combing he won't go.
"Eee! Phooey!" say the neat,
"That dreadful Scruffypete!"

≈   ≈   ≈

The Tale of Wicked Frederick

Young Frederick was a wicked lout.
He pulled the wings of houseflies out.
He smashed up chairs in wicked rages,
and murdered little birds in cages.
Another of his nasty tricks
was killing cats with heavy bricks,
and, oh, I tell you, it's perverse,
he used a whip to strike his nurse!

A great big dog stood at the spout
and drank the water flowing out.
Our Frederick then crept up unseen,
his whip in hand, his plan was mean.
He whipped the dog, which howled in pain,
yet Frederick kicked and struck again.
The dog then sank his sharp white teeth
through shoe and skin to blood beneath
and Frederick with a blood-stained sock
screamed loud and wept in pain and shock.
The dog, however, chose to fly,
his tail, his head, the whip held high.

In bed must Frederick now remain,
his foot has caused him dreadful pain.
The doctor sits there, poker-faced.
The medicine has a nasty taste.
The dog sits down in Frederick's place
and eats the sausage, leaves no trace.
To quench his thirst he drinks the wine,
And eats the cake and finds it fine.
He's put the whip nearby, you see,
and guards it very carefully.

෨ ෨ ෨

The Very Sad Story of the Matches

Paulina was alone today.
Her parents both had gone away
just for an hour. She sang with glee –
the Lady of the House was she –
and looked around for what to do,
for something grown-up, something new.
A box of matches then she spied.
"Oh, what a lovely game," she cried,
"I'll strike a match to make a light
just like my mother does. That's right!"

But Puss and Pounce down on the mat
throw up their furry paws at that.
"Your Father said you must not touch.
Miaow, miaow, it is too much!
Miaow, miaow, they're not for games!
Stop that or you'll go up in flames!"

This good advice Paulina spurns
and watches how the matchstick burns.
It flickers, crackles, loud and bright.
Paulina likes the pretty light.
Because the fire excites her so,
she can't stop running to and fro.

But Puss and Pounce down on the mat
throw up their furry paws at that.
"Your Mother said you must not touch.
Miaow, miaow, it is too much!
Miaow, miaow, they're not for games!
Stop that or you'll go up in flames!"

Oh dear, her dress has caught alight,
her pinafore is burning bright,
her hand's on fire, her arm, her hair,
and now she's burning everywhere.

But Puss and Pounce down on the mat
begin to caterwaul at that.
"Help! Oh, help! The child's on fire!
Can no one help? Her state is dire!
Miaow, miaow, it isn't games!
The whole Paulina is in flames."

The flames consume the child outright.
The whole Paulina burns up quite
until the only residues
are heaps of ash and two red shoes.

But Puss and Pounce, the little dears,
can only sit and cry sad tears,
"Miaow, miao, miao, miaow,
where are the poor, poor parents now?
and weeping cataracts of woe
make rivers on the floor below.

❧   ❧   ❧

The Tale of the Black Boys

Outside the town there took a stroll
a Moor with skin as black as coal.
The sunshine made his head too hot,
his parasol would shade the spot.
Then came young Lewis running by,
his banner held up very high,
while Jasper joined him at a pace
and brought some bread to feed his face.
And William likewise was not slow,
he had a big round hoop to throw.
They laughed and shouted out, all three,
the little Moor caused them such glee
because as black as ink was he.

Great Nicholas was on the spot
at once with ink in his big pot.
He spoke, "Now children, what I say
is leave the Moor in peace, okay!
What do you think that he could do
to be not black but white like you?"
The three just laughed, showed no dismay
(it did not hurt to disobey).
They laughed much louder than before
about the hapless coal-black Moor.

Great Nicholas grew truly wild
and took in hand each mocking child.
The picture shows his hold was firm
on Jasper, who was quick to squirm,

on William and on Lewis too –
on head and arm and jacket blue.
Into the ink he thrust in ire,
in spite of Jasper screaming "Fire!",
over their heads in blackest ink
Nicholas dunked them, made them sink.

And here you see how black they are,
much blacker than the Moor by far!
The Moor in front in sunshine bright,
behind him three as black as night,
and if they had not mocked the Moor
they'd still be white, of that I'm sure.

୧ଦ   ୧ଦ   ୧ଦ

The Story of the Bold Brave Hunter

The bold brave hunting man put on
his new green jacket and was gone
with satchel, powder-flask and gun
across the fields out in the sun.

He wore his glasses on his nose.
To shoot the hare he did propose.

The hare sits still behind some leaves,
laughs at the hunter's bright green sleeves.

The sun shone bright; the heat was great.
The shotgun was a heavy weight.
He lay down on the soft green hill.
The little hare was watching still
and as the hunter snored and slept
our hare across the meadow crept;
he took the glasses and the gun
without a sound, and planned some fun.

The hare has put the glasses on
his furry nose and thereupon
he wants to try a shotgun burst.

The hunter wakes now, fears the worst.
He turns to run off with a yelp,
"Oh, help me someone! Help! Oh, help!"

And so the bold brave hunter fled.
At last he reached the well; in dread

he jumped right in, his need was great.
The hare was shooting pretty straight.

The hunter's wife looked out to see
just what was up; the cup of tea
there in her hand was shot in two.
She cried, "Oh dear! Oh, what a do!"

Hard by the well had hid for fun
the hare's small child, the little bun'.
There in the long green grass he froze.
The hot tea spilled upon his nose.
He cried, "Who's burning me? It's sore!"
And had the teaspoon in his paw.

๛   ๛   ๛

The Story of the Boy Who Sucked his Thumb

"Conrad," said his mother, "Dear,
I'll go out but you'll stay here.
Do be good and do no wrong
till I'm back. I won't be long.
And I warn you, I implore,
You must suck your thumb no more."

"To the child that perseveres
comes the tailor with his shears,
cuts small boys like paper through,
two thumbs off with no ado."
Conrad's mother went, and then
Conrad sucked his thumb again.

Wham! The door is opened wide.
With a leap appears inside
that dread tailor; he has come
to the boy that sucks his thumb.
Oh dear! Just a snap and snip,
those sharp shears go twice clip clip,
Conrad's thumbs are off and gone.
Conrad screams and looks quite wan.

Conrad's looking very sad
and his mother won't be glad.
Without thumbs he's standing there.
He can't find them anywhere.

The Story of Fidgety Philip

"At the table we sit still!
Do you think that Philip will?"
Father spoke in earnest tone
(to which he was very prone).
Philip's mother simply stared
at the meal she had prepared.
Philip did not choose to hear
earnest words meant for his ear.
He scuffled
and shuffled,
he wriggled,
and jiggled,
back and forth he rocked the chair.
"Philip, this I cannot bear!"

Look, dear children, take a look
at the picture in the book,
see what comes of such hoo-ha:
Philip rocks the chair too far,
rocks it till it starts to fall.
He can't stop it, not at all.

Philip grabs the tablecloth –
it's no help. The bowl of broth,
dishes, bottle, spoons and forks
fall with Philip. Father gawks.
Philip's Mother still just stared:
where's the meal she had prepared?

Philip's nowhere to be seen
and the table's bare and clean.
Father's meal he waited for
rolls around down on the floor.
Broth and bread and wine and all
shared in Philip's sudden fall.
Cracked through is the soup tureen –
Philip's parents view the scene.
Both are angry as can be,
they'll stay hungry, you can see.

෨෨ ෨෨ ෨෨

The Story of No-Soup-Norman

Our Norman he was fat and round,
a healthy boy and very sound,
his cheeks were plump and pink and bright,
he ate his soup up, as is right.
Till one day he began to crow,
"I don't want any soup, no, no!
I do not want my soup, I don't!
I will not eat my soup, I won't!"

Just one day later – see his state –
our Norman had lost lots of weight
but once more he would only crow,
"I don't want any soup, no, no!
I do not want my soup, I don't!
I will not eat my soup, I won't!"

Then on day three – it does look bleak –
our Norman is now thin and weak.
and when the soup was served, you know,
again our Norman had to crow,
"I don't want any soup, no, no!
I do not want my soup, I don't!
I will not eat my soup, I won't!"

And on day four – so hard is fate –
our Norman weighed a pennyweight,
his arms and legs just like a thread –
and on day five he was quite dead.

৯৹ ৽৹ ৽৹

The Story of Harry Head-in-a-Cloud

Harry walked to school each day,
without looking at the way,
always gazing at the sky,
clouds and swallows flying by,
never at his own two feet
where they walked along the street.
Many people said aloud,
"Harry's head is in a cloud!"

Following a scent, a dog,
Harry walking at a jog,
eye on the sky,

there came no cry,
"Harry! look!" I think you've guessed
what happened next.
Wham! and whoops! Tripped in mid-stride,
dog and Harry side by side.

Harry walked along the quay,
schoolbag in his hand and he,
looking at the deep blue sky
where the swifts and swallows fly,
did not notice that his way
took him straight towards the bay
where three little fishes gazed,
open-mouthed and quite amazed.

One more step and Harry fell
headfirst deep into the swell.
Those three fishes, very scared,
to a safer place repaired.

What good luck! For there came two
men who knew just what to do,
straight away they were so quick,
fished out Harry with a stick.

Look! He stands there dripping wet.
That's no fun at all, I bet.
Water running from his hair
in his eyes and everywhere,
down each leg into each shoe,
and he's frozen through and through.

And the fishes, yes, those three,
back in place along the quay,
stretch their heads above the tide.
Hear them laughing far and wide!
Hear their laughter all the day!
And the schoolbag floats away.

⁓   ⁓   ⁓

The Story of Flying Robert

When it's pouring down with rain
and the wind's a hurricane
little girls and little boys
stay indoors with books and toys.
Robert thought, however, "No!
Outdoors must be great. I'll go!"
Through the field – oh what delight! –
holding his umbrella tight.

How the hurricane did blow!
There the tree is bent down low.
The umbrella in the gale
lifts with Robert who must sail
into the air, so far, so high
no one hears his startled cry.
Look! The clouds are very near
and his hat is flying clear.

Robert and umbrella too
fly on to the clouds and through,
further still his hat must fly
till it bumps into the sky.
Where the wind with Robert blows,
where he's got to, no one knows.

෨෨ ෨෨ ෨෨

Afterword

DER STRUWWELPETER, "Merry stories and funny pictures for children between three and six years," by Dr. Heinrich Hoffmann, in English speaking countries mostly know as "Slovenly Peter" or "Shock-Headed Peter," is the best known German children's book. First published in Frankfurt in 1845, it soon conquered the children's book market of the world not only with dozens of translations but also literally hundreds of imitations, adaptations, take-offs and parodies. A first anonymous English translation of the book was published in 1848 and a different, also anonymous, American one in New York in 1849. Today, translations into close to one hundred different languages and dialects, include Hebrew, Yiddish, Afrikaans, Lithuanian, Estonian, Latvian, Mauritian Creole, Reunionese Creole, Chinese, Japanese, Esperanto, ancient and modern Greek, and, of course, Latin. These testify to the book's lasting appeal, even though its pedagogical content, firmly rooted in nineteenth-century educational concepts, may perhaps no longer be considered modern and adequate. Recently, the book has again become popular through the parodistic "junk opera" stage adaptation, "Shockheaded Peter," which enjoys an enthusiastic reception world-wide.

Surprisingly, the book has seen no less than five complete, published versions in Latin, originating not only in *Struwwelpeter's* homeland, but also in England, Italy and Switzerland. These translations differ from their counterparts in other languages in several respects. For one thing, they are not directed at a juvenile audience "between three and six years," as Hoffmann meant the book to be. They thus have no explicit pedagogical intention. Made by professional Latinists as a tongue-in-cheek philological exercise and, as the translator of the present version called it, "for the sheer fun of it," their didactic purpose limits itself to the teaching and the enjoyment of Latin.

The history of Latin *Struwwelpeter* translations starts with a version which appeared in England (Rouse 1934), where the book enjoyed great popularity. Written in couplets of thirteen, and occasionally seven syllables, *The Latin Struwwelpeter* imitates medieval Latin poetical patterns, and is based not on the German original, but on the first English translation of 1848. A few lines from "The Story of Little Suck-a-Thumb" from this English version can provide a comparative reference for Rouse's Latin version.

> One day, Mamma said "Conrad dear,
> I must go out and leave you here.
> But mind now, Conrad, what I say,
> Don't suck your thumb while I'm away.
> The great tall tailor always comes
> To little boys that suck their thumbs;
> And ere they dream what he's about,
> He takes his great sharp scissors out
> And cuts their thumbs clean off – and then,
> You know, they never grow again."

Sugipollex

Aliquando filium mater allocuta,

71

"Foras eo, fili mi, cuncta domi tuta:
Aufer tu quisquilias, aufer istas nugas:
Moneo praecipue pollicem ne sugas.
Nam si sugunt pollices pueri profecto
Sartor vestiarius praesto subest tecto:
Dumque visum subitum miseri mirantur,
Forcipem grandissimam stringit properanter,
Amputatque pollices, qui decreto fati
Nunquam crescent iterum semel amputati."

৩০ ৩০ ৩০

This first Latin translation was followed by one published by H. J. Schmidt in Germany in 1938, *Petrus Hirsutus*. It, too, fits to the mould of medieval Latin verse, this time adopting the familiar meter of couplets in seven or eight syllables, so well know from the lyrics of the *Vagantes*, and, incidentally, closer to the rhythm of Hoffmann's original German. Schmidt's translation of the passage above reads as follows:

De Conrado pollices lambente

Mater suo Conrado
"Ego, inquit, exeo;
Interim sis bono more,
nunquam pollex sit in ore;
sartor nam cum forfice
advolat citissime,
desecabit acies
cito tuos pollices!"
Haec locuta abiit
et Conradus annuit.

৩০ ৩০ ৩০

Since the source of this and all other Latin translations is the German original, it deserves to be quoted here too.

"Konrad," sprach die Frau Mama,
"Ich geh aus und du bleibst da.
Sei hübsch ordentlich und fromm,
Bis nach Haus ich wieder komm.
Und vor allem, Konrad, hör!
Lutsche nicht am Daumen mehr;
Denn der Schneider mit der Scher
Kommt sonst ganz geschwind daher,
Und die Daumen schneidet er
Ab, als ob Papier es wär."

৩০ ৩০ ৩০

Next in line is Peter Wiesmann's translation (1954, typescript 1953), which we are pleased to present here with the kind permission of Tschudy Publishers, St. Gallen, Switzerland. The author of *Petrus Hirsutus* was a dedicated classical philologist. Born in Herisau (Switzerland) in 1904, he studied Latin and Greek at the University of Zurich, where he also earned a PhD in classical philology. He then taught both languages in secondary schools in Zurich and Chur from 1928 until 1980. Beside *Struwwelpeter*, Wiesmann also translated other texts into Latin, such as student songs by the German poet Victor von Scheffel and poems by Christian Morgenstern. Wiesmann died in 1981.

His translation was made independently from the two versions above. It, too, traces its form to the songs of the *Vagantes*, such as we know them from the *Carmina Burana*. In his afterword, Wiesmann writes that he modeled his style according to "G. Merten's congenial translation of Max und Moritz" (Merten, 1932). As a teacher, Wiesmann aimed his translation explicitly at Latin students, and, realistically – even then! – "those who are no longer as proficient in Latin." Thus his philologically accurate and stylistically elegant translation may well be more easily accessible to modern readers of Latin than the other versions. This makes it an excellent candidate for republication in this edition. The relevant passage from "De puero, qui pollices sugebat, fabula" reads:

> "Tu, Conrade, mi parebis,
> me absente remanebis!"
> dixit mater, "dum sum foris,
> opto, sis modesti moris.
> Audi tu, Conrade, imprimis:
> pollices ne sugas nimis!
> Nam cum forfice venturum
> pollicesque resecturum
> vestificum, ut papyrum,
> tibi dico, – non est mirum."

❦   ❦   ❦

Eduard Bornemann began his translation (*Petrulus Hirrutus*) as a revision of Schmidt's 1938 version (see above), but soon decided to make his own. As far as his style is concerned, he tells us that while his model is the poetry of the Latin Middle Ages, his "schoolmaster's heart, anchored in Antiquity" lead him to shun certain "liberties of post classical Latin," especially with regard to syntax and meter. His version, first published in 1956, has become the best know Latin one (last published in Walter Sauer 1994). The beginning lines from "De Philippo, puero oscillaci, fibula" are:

> Mater suo Conrado:
> "Remanes, dum exeo.
> Probus sis absente me!
> Sed imprimis hortor te:
> Cave rursus pollicem
> sugas, aut huc forficem
> tractans sartor est venturus
> ilicoque desecturus
> tuos pollices – securus,
> quasi sit papyrus purus."

❦   ❦   ❦

Compared to Bornemann's version, Ugo Enrico Paoli's translation, entitled *Petrus Ericius* (1960), is consistently classical. With the exception of the

"Prooemium," which is written in elegiac distichs, he chose hexameters as the metrical form, and made his story "Mos turpis sugendi pollicis qua poena luatur" begin in the following way:

"Me breviter, Conrado, foras exire necesse est;
At tu," mater ait, "manes bonus atque quietus,
Dum redeam, atque illud, quod mater praecipit, audi:
Foede te digitos labiis exsugere nolo.
Ne subito veniens praeacuta forfice sartor
Pollicem utrumque secet, veluti sit charta; memento."

Our comparative journey through five different Latin versions of "Die Geschichte vom Daumenlutscher" / "The Story of Little Suck-a-Thumb" can be complemented by the isolated translation of the story of "Conradus pollicilingus" by Wilfried (Valahfridus) Stroh (1993):

Mater dixerat Conrado:
'mane, ego foras uado.
tu piorum et proborum,
dum redibo, esto morum.
sed praecipue, Conrade:
pollices ne lingua rade!
aut cum forfice armatus
sartor ueniet citatus
pollicesque amputabit,
uelut chartas qui secabit'.

Finally, a version by Franz Schlosser from his hitherto unpublished *Petrulus Hirsutus* can be quoted as well:

Mater dixit Conrado:
"Remanes, dum abeo!
Probum esse velim te
Puerum absente me.
Et hanc unum tene rem:
Cave sugas pollicem –
Aut te viset praeditus
Forfice vestificus,
Pollice ut orbet te
Eo crudelissime!"

Heinrich Hoffmann's *Struwwelpeter* can be called a true children's classic. Its Latin translations certainly support this claim in more senses than one.

The text of Wiesmann's translation follows the edition of 1954. The book is accompanied by Heinrich Hoffmann's own illustrations. An anonymous English translation accompanies the German; a new English translation by Ann E. Wild appears as an appendix.

Works cited:

Bornemann, Eduard, 1956. *Petrulus Hirrutus "Der Struwwelpeter" sive Fabulae lepidae et picturae iocosae quas invenit ac depinxit Henricus Hoffmann doctor medicinae. Picturas secundum Hoffmanni exemplar delineavit et lignis incidit Fridericus Kredel. Versiculos in sermonem Latinum transtulit Eduardus Bornemann.* Francofurti Moenani: Rütten & Loening.

Merten, Gotthold A. L., 1932. *Max et Moritz facinorum puerilia septem dolis fraudibusque peracta ex inventione Guilelmi Busch poetae pictoribusque in sermonem Latinum conversa a versicatore sereno.* Monachii: Braun & Schneider.

Hoffmann, Heinrich, 1845. *Lustige Geschichten und drollige Bilder.* Frankfurt: Literarische Anstalt (J. Rütten).

Hoffmann, Heinrich, 1848. *The English Struwwelpeter. Pretty Stories and Funny Pictures.* Leipsic [sic]: Volckmar.

[Hoffmann, Heinrich], 1849. *Slovenly Peter; or Pleasant Stories and Funny Pictures.* New York: Town.

Hoffmann, Heinrich, 1859. *Der Struwwelpeter. Lustige Geschichten und drollige Bilder.* Frankfurt: Rütten & Loening.

Paoli, Ugo Enrico, 1960. *Petrus Ericius (Struwwelpeter). Lepidae historiolae ab Hugone Henrico Paoli Latinis versibus enarratae.* Firenze: Le Monnier; Bern: Francke.

Rouse, W[illiam] H[enry] D[enham], 1934. *The Latin Struwwelpeter.* London and Glasgow: Blackie & Son.

Sauer, Walter, 1994. *Der Struwwelpeter polyglott.* München: dtv.

Schlosser, Franz, *Petrulus Hirsutus. Latine redditus lineamentisque ornatus.* Ms., Waldsee (s.d.).

Schmidt, H[ans] J[ürgen], 1938. *Petrus Hirsutus seu fabulae iocosae ac imagines ridiculae per Dr. Henricus Hoffmann in linguam latinam travestitae per H. J. Schmidt. Illustrationes secundum primam denuo sunt pictae ac ligno incisae per Fridericum Kredel.* Potsdam: Rütten & Loening.

Stroh, Valahfridus, 1993. *Conradus pollicilingus (e D.ris Henrici Hoffmann libro c.t. Der Struwwelpeter.* In: Academiae Latinitati Fovendae Octavus Conventus, *Carmina.* Antwerpen und Leuven, 55–61.

Wiesmann, Peter, 1954. *Petrus Hirsutus vel fabulae iocosae lepidis imagunculis auctae secundum editionem primam denuo ab Alfredo Kobel delineatis ex inventione Doctoris Henrici Hoffmann in sermonem Latinum conversae ab Petro Wiesmann.* St. Gallen: Tschudy.

Running Latin-English Glossary

Praefatio
faveo, -ere: to favor
liberi, -orum, m.pl.: children
festum, -i, n.: holiday
modestus, -a, -um: good, obedient
ius, iuris, n.: soup
probus, -a, -um: good, obedient
fruor, -ui: to enjoy, to eat
obliviscor, -isci: to forget
resideo, -ere: to sit
deliciae, -arum, f. pl.: fine things, toys
affero, -ferre: to bring
imagincula, -ae, f.: picture

De Petro
hirsutus, -a, -um: shaggy, shock-headed
constituo, -ere: to put
quotannis (adv.): every year
idem: same
unguis, -is, m.: fingernail
recido, -ere: to cut
crinis, -is, m.: hair
pecto, -are: to comb

De Frederico
teter, -tra, -trum: nasty, hideous
nefarius, -a, -um: nefarious, naughty
scelestus, -a, -um: wicked
funestus, -a, -um: dirty
murus, -i, m.: wall, house
musca, -ae, f.: fly
capio, -ere: to catch
ala, -ae, f.: wing
eripio, -ere: to tear out
neco, -are: to kill, destroy
sella, -ae, f.: chair
avis, -is, f.: bird
felis, -is, f.: cat
clades, -is, f.: terror
quin: even
oppugno, -are: to beat
nec non: also
flagello, -are: to whip
soror, -oris, f.: sister
fons, -tis, m.: well
quondam (adv.): once
sto, -are: to stand
immanis, -e: big, enormous
haurio, -ire: to drink

canis, -is, m.: dog
lingua, -ae, f.: tongue
clam (adv.): secretly
accedo, -ere: to approach
manus, -us, f.: hand
flagellum, -i, n.: whip
gero, -ere: to carry
ferio, -ire: to beat
etsi (conj.): although
latro, -are: to bark
magis: more
iterum: again
calco, -are: to kick
crus, -uris, n.: thigh
corripio, -ere: to seize
cruor, -oris, m.: blood
mico, -ere: to splash
alte (adv.): high
pessimus, -a, -um: very bad
clarissimus, -a, -um: very loud
domum (adv.): home(ward)
revertor, -i: to return
os, oris, n.: mouth
flagrum, -i, n.: whip
recondo, -ere: to lay
lectus, -i, m.: bed
cubile, -is, n.: bed, resting place
amarus, -a, -um: bitter
medicamen, -inis, n.: medicine
libum, -i, n.: cake
comedo, -ere: to eat
hepaticus botulus, -i, m.: liverwurst
bibo, -ere: to drink
potulus, -i, m: cup
diligenter (adv.): carefully
custodio, -ire: to watch

De flammiferis
conclave, -is, n.: room
salio, -ire: to hop, to jump
conspicio, -ere: to see, to behold
miser, -era, -erum: unfortunate
mensula, -ae, f.: little table
flammiferum, -i, n.: match
Pol (interj., abbr.): by Pollux; wow!
virgula, -ae, f.: little stick
incendio, -ere: to light
conor, -ari: to try, to undertake
affectus (-a, -um) cura: seized by grief
tollo, -ere: to lift up, to raise
feles, -is, f.: cat

crus, -ris, n.: thigh, paw
sublatus, -a, -um (tollo): raised
moneo, -ere: to admonish
veto, -are: to forbid
vagio, -ere: to whine
interitus, -us, m.: destruction
paro, -are: to prepare
deflagro, -are: to burn to death
praebeo (-ere) aures: to listen
lignum, -i, n.: (kindling) wood
fulgeo, -ere: to shine, to sparkle
crepo, -are: to rattle
tremulus, -a, -um: crackling
imaguncula, -ae, f.: little picture
laetitia, -ae, f.: happiness, joy
illuc et huc (adv.): here and there,
   to and fro
atrium, -ii, n.: room
abicio, -icere: to throw away
tunica, -ae, f.: dress
capesso, -ere: to seize
praecinctorium, -i, n.: apron
ardesco, -ere: to catch fire
crinis, -is, m.: hair
exuro, -ere: to burn
quin (conj.): even
corripio, -ere: to seize
ambo, -ae, -o: both
vagitus, -us, m.: whining
opem (ops) fero (ferre): to help
celeriter (adv.): quickly
crudeliter (adv.): cruelly
huic (adv.): here
incendium, -i, n.: fire
uro, -ere: to burn to death
supersum, -esse: to be left
acervus, -i, m.: pile
cinis, -eris, m.: ash
nisi (adv.): except
ruber, -bra, brum: red
solea, -ae, f.: sandal, shoe
pauper, -is: poor
adsideo, -ere: to sit by
eiulo, -are: to cry
fluo, -ere: to flow
rivulus, -i, m.: little river, creek
pratum, -i, n.: meadow

De pueris
it (eo, ire): he is going
nigerrimus, -i, m.: a very black man
torreo, -ere: to burn, to scorch
umbella, -ae, f.: umbrella
calor, -oris, m.: (summer) heat

amoveo, -ere: to take away
vexillum, -i, n.: little flag
accurro, -ere: to rush to the scene
spira, -ae, f.: twisted band, pretzel
celeritas, -atis, f.: speed
mirus, -a, -um: amazing
trochus, -i, m.: hoop
haud: not exactly
praetereo, -ire: to walk by
clamo, -are: to shout
os, -ris, n.: face
illudo, -ere: to make fun of
atramentum, -i, n.: ink
pareo, -ere: to obey
Maurus, -i, m.: moor, African
afficio, -ere: to treat
eodem (pron.): (of) the same
pudor, -oris, m.: shame
sentio, -ire: to feel
gaudium, -ii, n.: joy, pleasure
rideo, -ere: to laugh
parvulus, -a, -um: small
vinco, -ere: to conquer, to overcome
imago, -inis, f.: picture
pingo, ere: to draw, to paint
poena, -ae, f.: punishment
ignarus, -a, -um: unknowing, unaware
quin etiam: even
cupa, -ae, f.: barrel; *here*: inkwell
universus, -a, -um: all
malus, -a, -um: naughty
submergo, -ere: to dip
licet: one can, it is possible
irrisor, -oris, m.: mocker
aliquanto (adv.): rather, somewhat
fulgeo, -ere: to shine
caput, -itis, n.: head
atratus, -a, -um: blackened
sequor, -i: to follow
denigratus, -a, -um: blackened
irrideo, -ere: to mock
vito, -are: to avoid

De saevo venatore
venator, -oris, m.: hunter
saevus, -a, -um: wild
astutus, -a, -um: clever, cunning
viridis, -e: green
vestis, -is, f.: suit, clothes
induo, -ere: to clothe, to put on
pera, -ae, f.: satchel
perspicillum, -i, n.: glasses, spectacles
lepusculus, -i, m.: little hare
nex, necis, f.: death

laturus, -a, -um (ferre, *fut. part.*): carry
lepus, -oris, m.: hare
folium, -i, n.: leaf
inopinans, -ntis: unsuspecting
ferveo, -ere: to be scorching hot
fio, fieri: to become
gravis, -e: heavy
recumbo, -ere: to lie down
sterto, -ere: to snore
clam (adv.): secretly
progredior, -gredi: to come forth
fugo, -ere: to flee
oculus, -i, m.: eye
munio, -ire: to arm
appeto, -ere: to approach
timesco, -ere: to become frightened
effugio, -ere: to flee, to escape
clamo, -are: to shout
obsecro, -are: implore; *here:* please!
succurro, -ere: to help
miser, -era, -erum: unfortunate
vis (*abl.* **vi):** strength
puteus, -i, m.: well
proicio, -ere: to throw
emitto, -ere: to shoot off
iaculum, -i, n.: gun (javelin)
en: behold!
coniux, -ugis, f.: wife
sorbeo, -ere: to sip
coffea, -ae, f.: coffee
ictus, -us, m.: shot
testa, -ae, f.: mug
uxor, -oris, f.: wife
timefactus, -a, -um: frightened
adspersus (adspergo): bespattered
uro, -ere: to burn
cochlear, -aris, n.: spoon
valde (adv.): very much
furo, -ere: to rage

De puero

remaneo, -ere: to stay home
dum (conj.): while
foris (adv.): not at home
opto, -are: to ask
mos, moris, m. (esse modesti moris): behavior (to be well behaved)
imprimis (adv.): first of all
pollex, -icis, m.: thumb
sugo, -ere: to suck
nimis (adv.): too much

forfex, -icis, f.: scissors
reseco, -are: to cut off
vestificus, -i, m.: tailor
papyrum, -i, n.: paper
non mirum: not surprising
claudo, -ere: to close
ianua, -ae, f.: door
denuo (adv.): again
subito (adv.): suddenly
recludo, -ere: to open
conspicio, -ere: to see
intro, -are: to enter
pupulus, -i, m.: little boy
digitus, -i, m.: finger
horrifice (adv.): in a horrible way
eiulo, -are: to wail
redeo, -ire: to come back
interim (adv.): in the meantime
gestum *from* **gero, -ere:** to happen

De Casparo

iusculum, -i, n.: broth, soup
validus, -a, -um: healthy
crassus, -a, -um: fat, chubby
pallidus, -a, -um: pale
rubeo, -ere: to be red
gena, -ae, f.: cheek
intersum, -esse: to be present
modeste (adv.): well-behaved
cena, -ae, f.: table, meal
quondam (adv.): once
cedo, -ere: to obey
edo, -ere: to eat
ullus, -a, -um: any
frustulum, -i, n.: bite, swallow
postridie (adv.): the next day
macer, -cra, -crum: meagre
debilis, -e: weak
peius (comp. malus): worse
cibus, -i, m.: food
appono, -ere: to put
tollo, -ere: to push away
denuo (adv.): again
nilum: nothing
filum, -i, n.: thread
semuncialis, -e: weighing half an ounce
mortem obeo (obire): to die

De Philippo

oscillo, -are: to rock
nonne (adv.): if not

placidus, -a, -um: quiet, still
decebit (decet): will be (is) proper
aio: to say
serenus, -a, -um: calm
vultus, -us, m.: face
deflecto, -ere: to change
circumspicio, -ere: to look around
crus, -ris, n.: thigh, leg
sella, -ae, f.: chair
videlicet: plainly
adspicio, -ere: to look
immodestus, -a, -um: unruly,
  disobedient
quidnam (pron.): what
postea (adv.): afterwards
insolenter (adv.): excessively
delabor, -i: to fall
retineo, -ere: to hold back
arripio, -ere: to seize, to grip
mantelium, -i, n.: tablecloth
nusquam (adv.): nowhere
cado, -ere: to fall
catillum, -i, n.: little plate
frustra (adv.): in vain, unsuccessfully
detego, -ere: to uncover
obruo, -ere: to cover, to bury
humi (adv.): to (on) the ground
decido, -ere: to fall down
frustum, -i, n.: bit, bite to eat
ius, iuris, n.: broth, soup
everto, -ere: to destroy
funditus (adv.): totally
patina, -ae, f.: bowl
peractus, -a, -um: ended

De Iohanne
ludus, -i, m.: school
nequeo, -ire: to be unable
nubes, -is, f.: cloud
hirundo, -inis, f.: swallow
subiaceo, -ere: to lie under
fugiebat (fugio, -ere): escaped him, he
  was not aware of
ludo, -ere: to mock
repente (adv.): suddenly
prudenter (adv.): carefully
fio, fieri: to happen
congredior, -i: to meet
labor, -i: to fall down
ripula, -ae, f.: river bank
capsula, -ae, f.: briefcase
sursum (adv.): up(wards)
gurges, -itis, m.: (depth of) water

tulit (ferre, *perf.*): he carried
ordinatim (adv.): in a row
gradus, -us, m.: step
perterreo, -ere: to become very
  frightened
in imum: at last
recondo, -ere: to hide
casu (abl.): by chance
procul (adv.): far
contus, -i, m.: pole
madefacio, -ere: to wet
en: behold!
Mehercle: by God (Hercules)!
risus, -us, m.: laughter
demano, -are: to pour down
frigeo, -ere: to be cold
illius omnes miseret: all pity him
adnato, -are: to swim by
porrigo, -ere: to stick out
diutissime (sup. adv.): a very long
  time

De Roberto
pluit: it is raining
strepitus, -us, m.: noise
ager, -gri, m.: field
fremitus, -us, m.: storm
domi (adv.): at home
displiceo, -ere: to displease
relinquo, -ere: to leave
diluvium, -i, n.: flood
parapluvia, -ae, f.: umbrella
strideo, -ere: to whistle
saevio, -ire: to rage
flecto, -ere: to bend
funestus, -a, -um: destructive,
  mournful
avolo, -are: to fly away
inclamo, -are: to cry for help
attingo, -ere: to touch
causia, -ae, f.: hat
amitto, -ere: to lose
vehor, -i: to fly
praegredior, -i: to go before, to pass
tegimentum, -i, n.: cover
tango, -ere: to touch
quo (adv.): where

"Living Latin" Titles
from Bolchazy-Carducci Publishers, Inc.

Vere, Virginia, Sanctus Nicolaus est!
Yes, Virginia there is a Santa Claus . . . in Latin!
32 pp. (2001) ISBN 0-86516-506-8

Cattus Petasatus
The Cat in the Hat in Latin
80 pp. (2000) ISBN 0-86516-472-X paperback
80 pp. (2000) ISBN 0-86516-471-1 hardbound

Quomodo invidiosulus nomine Grinchus
How the Grinch Stole Christmas in Latin
64 pp. (1998) ISBN 0-86516-420-7 paperback
64 pp. (1998) ISBN 0-86516-419-3 hardbound

Arbor alma
The Giving Tree in Latin
72 pp. (2002) ISBN 0-86516-499-1 hardbound

Makita
(original French story, 1936; Latin translation,
1997 by Melissa Foundation, Brussels)
175 pp. + 18 b&w illustrations (2001) ISBN 0-86516-013-6 paperback

Tonight They All Dance
92 Latin & English Haiku
(1999) ISBN 0-86516-440-1 paperback
(1999) ISBN 0-86516-441-X hardbound

Conversational Latin
for Oral Proficiency
256 pp. (2nd edition 1997) ISBN 0-86516-381-2 paperback
(2000) ISBN 0-86516-475-4 cassette

Latin Proverbs
Wisdom from Ancient to Modern Times
iv + 277 pp. (Forthcoming 2002) ISBN 0-86516-544-0 paperback

Words of Wisdom (CD)
From the Ancients, 1000 Latin Proverbs
(2000) ISBN 0-86516-502-5 CD-ROM

Visit us at: www.bolchazy.com